Museum Kittens

the real museum cats – HW

For Max and Bette - SL

STRIPES PUBLISHING LIMITED
An imprint of the Little Tiger Group
1 Coda Studios, 189 Munster Road,
London SW6 6AW

A paperback original
First published in Great Britain in 2020

Text copyright © Holly Webb, 2020
Illustrations copyright © Sarah Lodge, 2020
Author photograph copyright © Charlotte Knee Photography

ISBN: 978-1-78895-187-6

MIX
Paper from
responsible sources
FSC
www.fsc.org   FSC® C020471

The Forest Stewardship Council® (FSC®) is a global, not-for-profit organization
dedicated to the promotion of responsible forest management worldwide. FSC®
defines standards based on agreed principles for responsible forest stewardship
that are supported by environmental, social, and economic stakeholders.
To learn more, visit www.fsc.org

10 9 8 7 6 5 4 3 2 1

Museum Kittens

The Midnight Visitor

HOLLY WEBB

Illustrated by Sarah Lodge

LiTTLE TiGER

LONDON

Museum

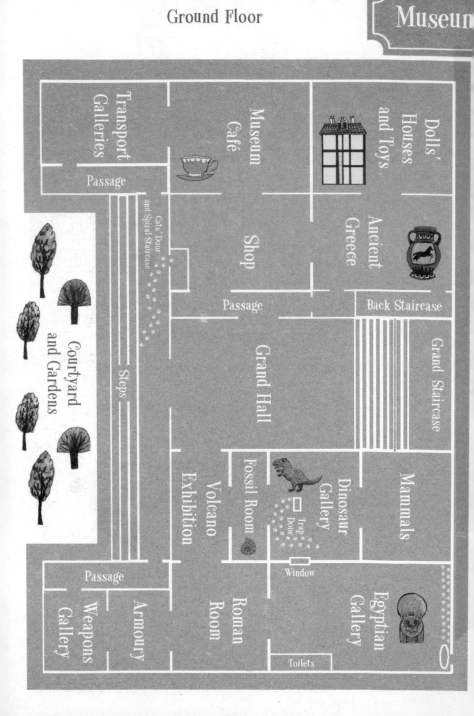

Transport Galleries

Passage

Museum Café

Dolls' Houses and Toys

Ancient Greece

Cats' Door and Spiral Staircase

Shop

Passage

Back Staircase

Grand Staircase

Courtyard and Gardens

Steps

Grand Hall

Fossil Room

Volcano Exhibition

Dinosaur Gallery

Trap Door

Mammals

Window

Egyptian Gallery

Passage

Weapons Gallery

Armoury

Roman Room

Toilets

Map

First Floor

China and Glass Room

Jewel Room

Russian Room

Passage

Polynesian Gallery

Japanese Gallery

Passage

Back Staircase

Maritime Gallery

Balcony

History of Cookery

Temporary Exhibition

Costume Gallery

Regency Room

Window

Passage

Ear Trumpet Collection*

Manuscript Room

Medieval Gallery

Musical Instruments

*Mrs Jane Martlesham Bequest

Chapter One

"Mrrrowww." Tasha rolled over and waved her tiny striped paws in the air. The wide stone steps that led up to the museum entrance were warm from the sun and she was so deliciously sleepy. There was a light breeze blowing off the river and she could hear gulls calling over the water.

"You're getting your fur dirty, Tasha,"

said a disapproving voice, and the tabby kitten opened one green eye to see who was talking to her. "Ma says we mustn't get our fur dirty – we should be clean and neat at all times."

"Oh hush, Bianca." Tasha closed her eye again, but it was no good. Her sister was still there – she could feel her. Bianca was blocking out the spring sunshine and now the afternoon felt dull and chilly.

"Ma says," Bianca insisted. She sat down next to Tasha and started to wash. She didn't need to – her white fur was spotless as always. Even her paw pads were perfectly pink and it looked as though she'd combed her beautiful whiskers.

Tasha rolled over and sprang up, peering over her shoulder at her grey and black tabby stripes. Bianca was right. She was covered in dust and her fur was sticking up all over the place. Half her whiskers seemed to be stuck together too – she wasn't sure how that had happened. She had gone exploring through the museum workshop earlier on. Perhaps she shouldn't have looked so closely at that pot of varnish. She stuck out her tongue to try and reach her sticky whiskers, but it didn't work.

"You are a disgrace to the museum," Bianca said, stopping mid wash with one paw in the air. "Just look at the state of you. Tch."

"I'm not!" Tasha said crossly. "We're supposed to be here to keep the mice and rats away. The rats don't care if my whiskers are tangled. It doesn't matter if I'm clean or not."

"Ma won't agree," Bianca purred, twitching her whiskers at a pair of visitors walking past them up the steps. "See? They thought I was adorable. They just said so. They didn't even notice you."

Tasha considered leaping on her sister's head and rolling her over in the dust.

Then she wouldn't be so perfect. But Tasha would only get into trouble. Ma might keep her downstairs in the cellars in the museum cats' den until bedtime, instead of letting her explore the museum and the courtyard and the gardens with the others.

"Come here," Bianca sighed, leaning over to lick the scruffy fur on Tasha's back. "I'll tidy you up."

Tasha's whiskers bristled as Bianca licked her fur straight. She sat hunched over with her ears flat back, letting out little outraged hisses.

"Don't make such a fuss! If you don't like being washed, you shouldn't get yourself in such a mess."

That did it! Tasha was going to have to

jump on her now, even if it meant staying in the cellars for weeks.

Just as she was about to pounce, their brother Boris hopped down the steps and bumped noses with Tasha. "Don't even *think* about doing that to me," he told Bianca with a yawn. "It's bad enough when Ma makes me wash my ears."

Bianca looked his ginger coat up and down and sniffed. "You're almost clean, I suppose." Then she sighed again at Tasha. All the bits of fur she'd licked clean and straight were starting to stick out already. "I give up," she muttered.

"Good! Oh look, more visitors."

All three kittens tried to look charming – sometimes the visitors had snacks to share. But as usual the visitors only made a fuss of Bianca. Tasha watched, wondering how her sister did it, and Boris settled down for a nap halfway off a step.

"White kittens are very unusual," Bianca purred as the visitors walked on up to the museum entrance. "You two are … common."

"Oi!" Boris opened one eye. "Ginger stripes are smart. Ma said so. I wouldn't want to be a white cat."

Bianca's blue eyes glittered. "And why not?" she hissed.

"Camouflage." Boris nodded knowingly. "I mean, you haven't got any. You stick out. Tasha and me can slink into the shadows and hide, because we've got stripes."

"Huh, I don't want to slink." Bianca sat up straighter and set her ears at the perkiest angle possible. "I am beautiful and I want everybody to see me." Then she frowned, her muzzle wrinkling as she looked at the dark dots spattering the terrace. "Ugh! It's *raining*! I shall get wet!" A large raindrop splashed down next to Bianca's delicate paws and her tail fluffed up in horror. The white kitten dashed up the steps and bolted across the terrace to the neat little door hidden behind one of the columns.

The museum building was very grand, with stone columns all along the front, and statues on either side of all the doors. Even the cats' door had its own little statue – a marble cat perched on the doorframe peering down. Its nose was almost rubbed away by hundreds of silky tails brushing past over the years.

As Bianca disappeared underneath the statue, a fluffy grey cat with a full fan of white whiskers appeared in the doorway and stepped out on to the terrace. Tasha thought about pretending not to have noticed her mother and darting off across the courtyard, but it wouldn't work. Smoke was a famous hunter and her green eyes were sharp. She'd know straightaway that Tasha had seen her.

"There's Ma looking for us," Boris groaned, and he and Tasha hopped up the steps and padded over to the grey cat.

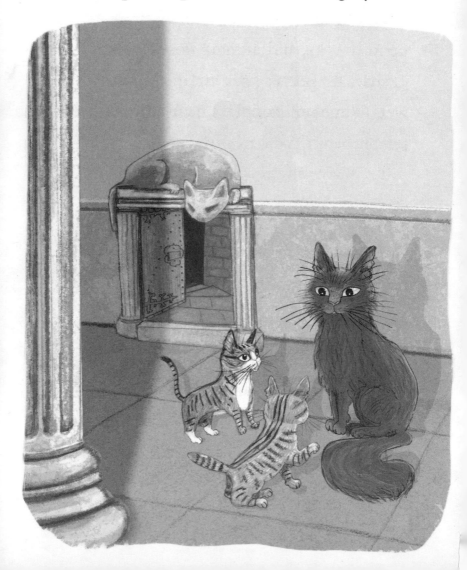

"Please can we stay out a bit longer?" Tasha pleaded. "It can't be even close to bedtime."

Smoke narrowed her eyes, peering up at the sky, and nudged noses with Tasha. "It's getting late, kitten. And it's wet. Come on inside, it's nearly time for supper. The Old Man brought us fish today as a treat."

The Old Man was one of the museum's guards and he was in charge of feeding the cats. He was grumpy and sometimes shouted at the kittens when they got in his way, but Ma said that was only because his legs hurt.

Boris's whiskers fanned out, trembling with excitement. "Fish! Come on, Tasha! We need to get down there first, before everyone nabs it."

The two kittens barged through the little door – they weren't quite tall enough for their tails to stroke the stone cat's nose yet – and pattered down the stairs to their shadowy home.

Chapter Two

The museum's cellar storerooms went on
a very long way underground. Even the
kittens' grandfather, the fearsome white
cat Ivan, hadn't explored them all. They
were full of boxes and chests and trunks
of ancient museum bits that almost
everyone had forgotten about.

The cats lived in the cellars at the
very front of the building, with a spiral

staircase leading up to the small door on the terrace. There was a sloping tunnel that led up into the Egyptian Gallery too, and opened out behind a very large and musty-smelling mummy case, as well as lots of other passages and chutes and hideaways that the cats used to get around.

Tasha, Bianca and Boris were asleep on an old tapestry full of holes, their tummies full of fish, with Smoke curled lovingly around them.

It was the dark of the night and the shower that had spattered down on the terrace that afternoon had turned into a storm. The wind rattled through the old chimneys and air ducts with shrill little whines and angry growls, and rain was lashing against the walls. Even safe underground, the kittens stirred and shifted uneasily in their sleep.

Tasha woke with a squeal as something banged loudly on the door at the top of the spiral staircase. The noise seemed to echo around the cellar and her fur prickled with fear. What was happening? That door should be shut tight.

There were cats out on duty in the museum, of course, prowling around the priceless objects in the galleries upstairs. They were on watch for mice and rats, or even burglars. But the cat guards knew to slide silently in and out of their den. This was an intruder!

"Stay here!" Smoke hissed, her green eyes glinting fiercely at her children in the soft light from the doorway. "I'll be back soon." Then she shot away, joining the tide of tabby and white and ginger fur surging out of the sleeping quarters towards that strange, suspicious noise.

The kittens stayed huddled together on the tapestry, feeling the warmth of their mother's body die away.

Tasha's tail was swishing anxiously

from side to side. "I want to see what's happening…"

"Ma said to stay," Bianca mewed.

"We could just look round the door," suggested Boris, standing up. "That wouldn't do any harm, would it?"

Tasha jumped up with an eager nod.

Bianca shuffled her paws worriedly, and then sprang down from the tapestry after Tasha and Boris. She didn't want to be left behind. All three kittens peered round the doorframe, trying to see further up the passage. In the dim light of the lamps they could just make out the spiral staircase, with shadowy cats standing sentinel all the way up the steps. They were as still as statues, but Tasha could hear the soft hiss of their breathing.

They couldn't see the door at the top.

"I want to know what it was!" Tasha's tail was flicking back and forth now, and her ears were flattened. "It's important, I know it is."

"No..." Bianca moaned, but the other two were already creeping along the passage.

Tasha started to weave her way up the staircase, between the cats. There were a few hisses of annoyance as her brother and sister followed, but no one stopped the three kittens as they pattered towards their mother and grandfather, who were standing together a few steps from the top.

"I thought you told them to stay in the den?" Old Ivan murmured to Smoke, his one eye narrowing, and she sighed.

"I did. I should have known you naughty kittens wouldn't listen. Now stay by me, you three, and *don't move*!" Then Smoke turned back to watching the heavy wooden door at the top of the stairs. The two cats on guard duty were pulling back the heavy bolts with their teeth.

Tasha shivered and pressed tight against her mother as the door opened a crack and the wind battered and shrieked against the dark timbers. All the cats on the stairs hissed, lowering their heads into the wind, feeling it lick their fur on end and tie their tails in knots.

The door swung fully open and a haze of damp air rushed in. Outside, the cats could see the rain lashing the flagstones on the terrace, each heavy drop striking up a little fountain as it landed. It was midnight-black out there, even the cats' night eyes were blind. The two cat guards took a cautious step forward and one of them bellowed, "Who goes there?"

"Identify yourself!" the other guard roared, not to be outdone.

There was a faint thickening of the darkness outside the door and then another cat appeared, a skinny old cat who looked even skinnier with the rain flattening his coat over his bones. His mackerel-tabby stripes seemed to melt into the shadows around the doorway. Something about him made the two guards fall back, pressing themselves respectfully against the doorframe to let him pass.

The cats on the stairs peered forward, staring at the skinny old tabby and waiting for him to speak.

But he didn't. He couldn't, Tasha and the others realized, because there was something in his mouth. A little saggy something, all black and bedraggled.

21

The old cat padded carefully down the steps until he reached Smoke and her kittens, and stood in front of her. Then he leaned down and laid the soggy ball of fur at her feet. He nodded slowly then turned round, pacing away up the stairs, and disappeared out into the rain-soaked night, still silent.

On the stairs, the wet ball of dark fur wriggled and sneezed and sat up, staring at Smoke and the kittens with emerald eyes.

"I'm Peter," squeaked the small black kitten, gazing nervously around at the rows and rows of cats. "Hello."

🐾 Chapter Three 🐾

"*Who was that?*" The whisper ran round the stairs, and the two guard cats hurried out on to the terrace to call the mackerel tabby back. But they returned looking downcast.

"No sign of him."

The little black kitten laid his ears flat and shuffled his paws. "He – er – he said he was taking me to my new home…"

A disapproving chorus echoed around the stairs at once.

"Here?"

"The little tadpole wants to stay!"

"Well, I'm not sure about that!"

"Quiet!" Old Ivan let out a loud, growly meow. "The museum is a home for all cats in need, you know that quite well. Besides, I've seen that mackerel-tabby fellow before. Around and about. He's a sensible creature. If he brought the kitten here, then here he stays."

Smoke came up beside Ivan and gently licked the black kitten's ears. "You must be so tired," she said to him gently. "Come back down to the cellars with us and sleep. The warmth from the hot-water pipes will dry your fur. You can tell us where you came from in the morning."

The rows of cats parted like a wave rolling back as she nudged the little black kitten down the stairs towards the cellars. She half lifted him on to the pile of old tapestries where Tasha and Bianca and Boris slept with her every night, and the three kittens followed. They lay down next to him, but it felt so odd curling up with their mother and a stranger.

Tasha lay there, her eyes half open, peering at the newcomer. She felt sorry for him, of course, being so cold and wet and lonely. But he didn't smell like a museum kitten.

When they woke up the next morning, the three kittens were snuggled up in Smoke's long grey fur, just like always. The black kitten was curled in a tiny ball at the very edge of the tapestries, all alone.

After breakfast and washing, Smoke tried to coax him to tell his story. Tasha sat beside her mother, watching eagerly. The most interesting part of living in a museum was all the stories that came with the treasures in the galleries, but a story she hadn't heard before was the very best kind. She was sure that the black kitten's adventures would be exciting. After all, he'd come from Out There.

But when the black kitten had licked breakfast off his whiskers at last and settled down to be questioned, he didn't seem to have a story to tell at all. He didn't know anything, except that he was called Peter, and that Herring, the old mackerel tabby, hadn't been his father or his grandfather. Just someone who had looked after him for as long he could remember and had brought him to the museum.

He sat in the middle of a circle of curious cats, his whiskers drooping as he failed to answer question after question.

"What was your mother's name?"

"Were you born here in the city?"

"Do you have any brothers or sisters?"

In the end, they gave up. There was no question of sending Peter away, of course. He would be a museum cat, like

all the others. But he was a strange one.
He didn't seem to fit, and the black kitten
knew it.

"Leave the poor creature alone," Old Ivan ordered. "If he doesn't know, then he doesn't know. Perhaps he'll remember in time." He fixed Tasha, Boris and Bianca with a stern glare. "You young ones must show him around." Tasha was never sure how her grandfather could look so much more fiercely with one eye than everyone else did with two, but he managed it. "Make him feel at home. Show him the ropes!"

"What ropes?" Boris muttered in Tasha's ear. "Does he mean the sailors' knot collection in the Maritime Gallery? Why do we have to show this scrawny kit those?"

"Shh!" Tasha hissed back. Even though both of Old Ivan's ears looked chewed and he was deaf in one ear, she was almost sure he'd heard Boris being rude. His whiskers were bristling.

Maybe Peter would like to see around the museum, she thought hopefully. Perhaps he'd like the same rooms she did. They could show him the fossilized fish, and the lion statues, and the shudderingly scary cat mummies in the Egyptian Gallery.

"Come on then," Bianca said a little haughtily – but not too haughtily because she was frightened of Grandpa Ivan too. No one knew exactly how he'd lost his eye and all those bits of his ears… "This way, you!"

❧ Chapter Four ❧

Peter obediently followed the three kittens through the galleries. Herring had told him that the museum was a strange place, full of treasures. "Though a lot of it's just old junk," the old tabby cat had added, chuckling. "Dusty old bones, not a scrap of meat on them."

Peter wasn't sure about the bones either, but the visitors certainly seemed to like them. Boris and Tasha and Bianca led him through the gaps under the floorboards and let him pop his head out of a tiny trapdoor in the middle of the Dinosaur Gallery. There were skeletons all around, but he could hardly see them for the crowds of people.

"What are they doing?" he whispered.

The three kittens stared at him. "Visiting," Tasha said at last. "It's what they do. They look at things."

"They take a lot of pictures," Bianca added. "Most of them take pictures of me," she added smugly.

Tasha rolled her eyes and saw Peter glance at her. "She's very spoilt," she whispered to him. "She loves having her picture taken."

"Come on!" Boris was already heading back down the tunnel. "I want to show him the swords."

"No," Bianca hissed. "The jewellery's much more interesting. There are six crowns," she added impressively to Peter, who nodded, wide-eyed.

"Boring sparkly stuff," Boris grunted, but he followed the others, slipping along the corridors and round the display cases to the Jewel Room.

"Keep hidden!" Bianca snapped. She batted Peter back into the shadows with one small white paw as he stopped to gaze up at the enormous marble staircase in

the Grand
Hall.

"We're not
really supposed
to be here," Tasha
explained as Peter blinked in
confusion. "We live down in the cellars –
upstairs is only for the visitors. The older
cats hunt the mice and the rats, but that's
at night when no one is around. The mice
and the rats are busier at night too, of
course. If we come upstairs during the
day, we have to stay out of sight. We're
allowed in the courtyard and the gardens,
though."

"I'm good at hiding," Peter said eagerly,
and Boris snorted.

"Not as if there's much of you to hide,"

he said, looking Peter over, and Peter scrunched himself down even smaller.

Tasha glared at her brother, but he didn't notice. "Come along," she told Peter. "We'll sneak up the back stairs, here. There's nowhere to hide on the Grand Staircase."

They peered down at the Jewel Room from above, squinting through a latticed air vent. The crowns and necklaces and diamond-encrusted eggs were all locked away in thick glass cases, but they still flashed and glittered in the sunlight from the tall windows.

They left
Bianca there
in the end, her
little pink nose
poking through the vent to get as close
to the jewels as she could. One of these
days she would have a diamond tiara of
her own, or a pearl necklace, perhaps.

"Now let's see the weapons," Boris
commanded, marching along a draughty
passage that led around the courtyard
to the next building. "Best room in the
whole place."

"Oh, it isn't!" Tasha stopped, staring
at him.

"What's your favourite?" Peter asked
her, and the tabby kitten's whiskers shook
as she tried to think.

"I'm not sure…" she admitted at last.
"I love them all."

"Typical," muttered Boris, looking back
at them both.

"I mean … the Egyptian Gallery …
and the dolls' houses … and then there's
the mosaics… I just can't choose."

"That's because you spend all your time
daydreaming about who those tatty old
things belonged to." Boris gave a big sigh.
"Come along, do. There! Look! Isn't that
impressive?"

The three
kittens scuttled
behind an open door and
peered round at the suits of armour
standing guard around the room. They
were eerie, Peter thought, waiting there
with their metal gauntlets on their
swords. He wouldn't like to peer under
the visors on those helmets, in case he
found something else looking back
at him.

"They're very grand," he agreed,
hoping to please Boris. But that only

meant he got a long tour, sneaking from case to case to inspect all of Boris's favourite swords. Boris was particularly keen on the Japanese ones and Peter had to stifle several yawns.

"Are you very bored?" Tasha whispered in his ear, in the middle of Boris's lecture on Samurai armour.

Peter twitched. He was, but he didn't like to say so. What if Tasha minded him saying her brother was boring?

"Boris, can you smell that?" Tasha sniffed thoughtfully. "What is it, do you think? Egg mayonnaise, maybe? Or tuna?"

"Sandwiches?" Boris abandoned the Samurai and gazed around the gallery, his whiskers stretched out like great white fans. "Just a minute." He crouched low and padded away, ears turning slowly as he tracked imaginary sandwiches.

"I couldn't smell anything," Peter said, frowning. He was rather proud of his sense of smell – he could sniff out a nice bit of bacon several dustbins away.

"Oh, neither could I. But you can always distract Boris with sandwiches. They're his favourite thing. Especially if he's sneaked them – he reckons they taste better if they're stolen. He's always raiding the bins in the museum café."

Peter wrinkled his muzzle. The tinned food that the Old Man had put down for them at breakfast had been so good, and there had been so much of it, even with all those cats to feed. He'd always

had not-quite-enough food, when he and
Herring had been wandering about the
city. He wondered if Boris had ever been
hungry. The ginger kitten certainly made
sure he got more than his fair share at
meal times – Peter didn't think he'd ever
seen anyone eat faster.

"Look out!" Tasha hissed suddenly,
interrupting his thoughts. "Visitors! We're
not supposed to be in here. Run!"

She skittered away into the shadows,
behind the massive armoured elephant.
Peter looked around wildly. He could
hear footsteps and voices getting closer
and closer. It sounded like a great
stampeding crowd. What if he was seen
in the galleries? Would he be thrown out
of the museum, after all old Herring had

done to get him here?

Peter stood frozen at the feet of the Samurai warrior, his tail fluffing to three times its size. Then, as the voices grew louder, he gave a tiny mew of panic, and shot upwards, inside the plated leather armour. If there was a ghostly warrior inside, it was going to get an awful shock...

He clung on tight to the ribbed metal, his heart thumping as the visitors talked and talked only a whisker or so away. What if they loved the Samurai soldiers as much as Boris did? He could be here for hours!

The sharp metal plates felt as if they were going to cut his claws in half. Were the visitors still there? The voices seemed to have moved further away – and now he could hardly hear them. Slowly, slowly, Peter crept back down and peeped out beneath the heavy armour-plated skirts.

The visitors had gone, but so had the other kittens.

"Tasha?" he called hopefully, glancing around the gallery. "Are you there? Boris?"

A faint echo whispered through the suits of armour, but that was all. Peter shuddered as the dark emptiness behind the visors seemed to turn towards him and scooted for the door.

He wasn't going to stay here to be eaten by long-dead warriors, he decided. If Tasha and Boris had abandoned him, he would just have to explore by himself.

Chapter Five

All through that first day, the older cats whispered as they curled up together, or set out on their guard duties. Even though Grandpa Ivan had said Peter must be allowed to stay, there was still a great deal of gossiping to be done. Whenever Peter padded past, exploring his new home, hissy little whispers followed him. The cats put their heads together and muttered.

No one knew how old the strange black kitten was, for a start. He was a great deal smaller than Boris, but then Boris was huge, everyone said so. He was nearly as tall as Bianca and Tasha but he was thinner, as though he'd never been properly fed. He kept appearing here and there, always hunched over or half hidden behind a box or a pile of papers. He was quiet too, now he knew that he had to be. He could slip through the passageways and galleries like a shadow.

"He's too quiet," Bianca said later that afternoon as the shadows were gathering along the terrace outside the Egyptian Gallery. "I don't like it. He's such a sly little thing. I expect he's off somewhere sniffing around where he isn't wanted."

"Or he's spying out the museum's treasures," Boris suggested. "What do we really know about that skinny old tabby cat who brought him here? He could be a master criminal and Peter's his cat on the inside."

Tasha was still feeling guilty about abandoning Peter earlier. She should have gone back to the Weapons Gallery to find him. Should she look for him now and say sorry? Or would that just make it worse? She was only half listening to Bianca and Boris, so she didn't argue with them for once. Afterwards she wished she had, because as soon as Bianca had wandered off to flutter her whiskers at a visitor and Boris had gone to enquire when supper would be, a small dark

shape stole out
from behind a
statue of a lion
goddess and slunk
away. Tasha sat
watching from the
terrace with her mouth
open, but all her words were frozen.

*It's just Bianca and Boris – you don't
need to mind them, I never do,* she should
have said. Or, *I wish I hadn't left you
behind in the Weapons Gallery. I didn't
mean to, I was just scared we'd get into
trouble...*

She tried to be friendly – that night she
left a space on their pile of tapestries for
the black kitten to sleep. But instead he
huddled himself up inside an old wooden

jewellery box, all on his own. Tasha lay there in the dark, watching him and worrying.

The black kitten didn't notice that Tasha was peering at him over Boris's fat ginger tail. He was squished into the tiny jewellery box, the worn velvet lining soft under his paws. He was quite comfortable and he wasn't hungry. He was warm and dry, and Old Ivan had said he could stay.

But he didn't belong. Not like the others. Clever funny Tasha, and Bianca who melted all the visitors' hearts. And Boris, who was obviously going to be the biggest, fiercest, most rat-scaring cat in the whole history of the museum.

Peter sniffed, and sighed, and turned round in the tiny, tiny box – which was quite difficult. Perhaps it would be better tomorrow, he thought hopefully, as his head nodded lower on to the edge of the box. Perhaps tomorrow things would be different...

"Are you sure you're even a cat?" Boris peered down, his whiskers brushing the little black kitten's nose. He was looking sideways at Bianca and Tasha, wanting them to laugh along.

"What?" Peter blinked. "Of course I'm a cat."

"Are you? Really? I mean you don't know anything else about yourself. Maybe you're a skinny little ferret." Boris sniggered, thinking that he was being very clever and funny. "Or perhaps you're a rat! I've seen rats bigger than you!"

Peter shuddered. He had seen rats too, while he was out on the streets with Herring. Their yellow teeth and glittering eyes would be stuck in his memory forever.

"Leave him alone," Tasha growled. "You aren't funny, Boris.

Maybe you're an elephant? Stop being mean."

Peter was still thinking about rats and hardly heard her. But he heard Bianca laughing, a high squeaky little laugh that made him feel hot and embarrassed and miserable all over. His ears flattened down and his tail drooped, and he skulked silently away from the three kittens.

"Off you go, rat cat!" Boris called after him, snorting with laughter, and Peter hung his head. He'd really thought that today might be better. Today was supposed to be the day that he fitted in. How could he ever be a real museum cat when he knew nothing about who he was, or where he came from? All the others had been born at the museum – they were never going to let him be one of them. Wherever he went in the galleries, there seemed to be a proper museum cat peering down its nose at him.

He couldn't stay.

Peter slunk through the Dinosaur Gallery like a tiny patch of shadow and crept into a room full of stuffed animals. None of the museum cats liked this room much – it smelled strange and there were too many large creatures with teeth. The enormous she-wolf just by the door made him feel quite shivery. But in here he had a good chance of being left alone to work out what he was going to do. He settled down behind a glass case with a sabre-toothed tiger in it and began to wash slowly. It helped him think.

Herring had told Peter that the
museum was a safe place, where cats
were well cared for, and Peter could see
that this was true. He had been very well
fed. He closed his eyes for a moment,

blissfully remembering the treat of cold chicken that the Old Man had put down as part of their supper the night before. It made his whiskers quivery just thinking about it. And he was warm and dry with a comfortable place to sleep. Even though he had woken up feeling as if the jewellery box had given him corners!

But it wasn't enough. Smoke licked his ears affectionately whenever she strolled past, but no one talked to him. No one curled up around him to keep him safe in the dark, the way Herring had. And before that, someone had loved him. Peter couldn't remember his mother or father, or his brothers and sisters, but he knew he must have had a family, once.

He almost remembered someone licking him gently as he fell asleep.

The museum was a place to stay, but that didn't make it a home. Peter stopped licking his paws and breathed out a tiny sigh. He didn't want to leave the good food and the warm bed and go back to wandering the streets. Especially not on his own.

But wasn't a home worth hunting for?

Chapter Six

Peter was still sitting behind the sabre-toothed tiger, trying to come up with a plan, when a scuffling noise made him jump. He peered out from behind the glass case, hoping that it wasn't one of the enormous rats that Boris had so enjoyed telling him about on their tour.

It wasn't a rat. Staring back at him with wide panicked eyes was Tasha, her fur all on end and her whiskers bristling.

"What's the matter?" he gasped. "Are you all right?" The tabby kitten looked terrified, as though something was after her. Peter glanced worriedly around the gallery, wondering what it could be.

"Oh… It's you." Tasha panted. The fur along her spine flattened down a little and she took a deep breath. "I thought… Oh dear." She padded her front paws up and down, looking embarrassed.

"Is someone chasing you?" Peter asked, his whiskers flicking anxiously back and forth.

Tasha shook her head slowly. "No…" She looked behind her and then edged a little closer to the tiger case. "Promise you won't tell the others?"

Peter felt something inside him swell up like a little balloon. A secret! Between him and Tasha!

"I promise," he said earnestly, hoping and hoping it wasn't some horrible trick that Boris or Bianca had put her up to.

"I'm-really-scared-of-the-wolf," Tasha said in a fast, muttery gabble.

"Oh…" Peter looked over at the entrance to the gallery, where the huge stuffed wolf stood on a high wooden block, baring her teeth. He could almost hear her growling from here, even though he knew she was stuffed. "Me too."

"Really?" Tasha said, sounding surprised and a little bit relieved. "I didn't think you would be. I mean, you've been a street cat – you've seen lots of scary things, I expect."

Peter nodded. "That's why I'm scared of the wolf – it looks exactly like the enormous German Shepherd that chased me and Herring for miles and miles one night. We only got away because we scrambled up a fire escape and hid behind some chimneys. The dog couldn't follow us up on to the roof, but we had to stay there until it got light."

"Uuuugggghhhh." Tasha shuddered and closed her eyes. "I don't even want to think about it."

"Sorry. I didn't mean to make it worse," Peter told her apologetically. Then he wrinkled his nose. "But why did you come in here, if you don't like the wolf?"

"To find you, of course." Tasha leaned forward and dabbed noses with him. Peter was so surprised he nearly darted back behind the sabre-toothed tiger.

"To find me?" he squeaked.

"Yes. I wanted to say I shouldn't have run off and left you in the Weapons Gallery yesterday, I'm ever so sorry. And I'm sorry that Boris is so horrible. He's my brother and I'm absolutely ashamed of him. And Bianca isn't much better."

"Oh…" Peter stared at her. He hadn't expected that at all.

"I think Boris might actually be a bit jealous," Tasha went on. "He's never lived outside the museum, or had any grand adventures. All he does is skulk around, trying to steal snacks."

"Um – I haven't had any grand adventures either," Peter pointed out humbly.

"Oh, but you have!" Tasha was practically bouncing up and down on her paws. "You arrived at the museum in the middle of a dark and stormy night! And no one knows where you came from!"

"Even I don't know," Peter said, gazing glumly at the floor. "It's horrible. Like I don't belong anywhere."

"Really? Is that how you feel?" Tasha's green eyes widened. "I thought it was exciting and wonderful and mysterious."

Peter sat up a little straighter and felt his whiskers curl a bit. "Mysterious?"

"Oh yes. I'm extremely jealous and I think Boris is too." Then she looked at him anxiously. "I knew Boris and Bianca were being horrible, but I never realized they were making you feel like you didn't belong here. I know everyone keeps whispering about you, but it's not only because you're new – and different! It's not up to them! Grandpa Ivan said the museum was for *every* cat. You … you are going to stay, aren't you? Do you like it enough to stay?" She ducked her head shyly. "Do you like *us*?"

"I *was* thinking about going," Peter admitted. "I was trying to make a plan. I don't know the city very well, you see. When we were travelling here, I just followed Herring. So I wasn't sure how to go about finding my real home."

"*This* is your real home," Tasha said firmly. "You *do* belong."

Peter shuffled his paws sadly. "But I'm so little and skinny," he muttered. "And there aren't any other black cats at the museum. No one's like me. And –" he looked around secretively and then whispered – "I've never caught a rat. Not even a mouse, actually."

"Oh well, neither have I," Tasha admitted. "We're not old enough, Ma says. There are rats in some of the galleries that are bigger than Boris."

Peter stared at her, not sure whether to be relieved or not.

"So Boris hasn't caught one either?" he asked.

"Nope. We've got a toy one that a little girl gave to Bianca. But it's got a tail made of feathers." Tasha rolled her eyes.

"The visitors are very strange sometimes. Imagine not knowing the difference between a mouse and a bird!"

"I thought you all must have done lots of guard work at the museum," Peter murmured, his eyes brightening.

"We're only just starting to learn," Tasha told him. "Sometimes Ma gives us lessons, and so does Grandpa Ivan, but he says we're absolutely useless. Look, if you did catch a rat, would it make you feel better?"

Peter swallowed hard, thinking of glittering eyes, sharp yellow teeth and whip like tails, but he nodded. "Yes."

Tasha nodded determinedly. "All right. Then that's what we'll do."

❧ Chapter Seven ❧

They'd been creeping stealthily in and out of the galleries for hours, searching for even a sniff of a rat, and Peter's paws were starting to ache. Luckily the Egyptian Gallery seemed to be clear of visitors just now. It was tea and cake time, Tasha had explained, when most of the visitors decided they needed to nip to the café for a little something to keep them going.

"Are you sure there are rats in the museum?" Peter asked, sitting down next to a huge pink granite lion for a rest.

"Oh yes." Tasha nodded firmly – and then she looked round all the statues and sighed. "They're always causing trouble. We see them in passageways every so often but they always scuttle off. They try and sneak in the kitchens of the museum café and eat the cakes, but the worst thing is, they eat the treasures sometimes too."

She leaned close to Peter and whispered darkly, "There's a beautiful silk kimono in the Japanese Gallery with cherry blossom and cherries embroidered all over it. Except if you look closely, it's covered in little holes where the rats nibbled the cherries right off!"

"But silk cherries don't taste of anything, do they?" Peter frowned.

"Of course not. But rats are too dim to work that out."

The two kittens didn't see the flicker of a long pink tail over in the corner behind a stone pharaoh. They didn't hear a sharp hiss of indrawn breath or the scurrying of paws as a very insulted rat hurried away to tell all his friends what he'd just heard.

Peter shook his head. "I don't think there are any rats left. Maybe your mother and grandfather and aunties and uncles are just such good rat-catchers, the rats have all gone? We haven't seen a single one. Not even a mouse either."

"Maybe." Tasha sighed. "We have been looking for ages." She glanced behind her to check no visitors were around, then she hopped up on to the lion's concrete plinth and settled in between his hind paws, where there was a comfy little nook. She slumped over the stone and looked down at Peter.

Peter watched her anxiously. They'd been chasing round the museum all afternoon and the tabby kitten looked grumpy. Perhaps she was wishing she hadn't offered to help? Perhaps she'd changed her mind and now she wanted him to go away?

Sadly he started to shuffle backwards away from Tasha and the pink stone lion, but then she leaned over the lion's paw and asked, "Where are you going? Why don't you come up here? This lion's nice to sit on, but he's chilly."

"Oh!" Peter's ears twitched back up, and he jumped on to the statue next to her.

"This is an Egyptian king, you know," Tasha told him chattily as he snuggled down next to her. "They liked cats. This one pretended he was a lion. Two lions, actually, there's another one of him over there."

"That's ... odd." Peter looked up at the lion's face. The statue was certainly very grand. But he wasn't sure how a king could think he was two huge cats at once.

"You'll get used to it. The museum's full of odd things. There's a statue over there with a human body and a cat's head.

No tail though, which is a bit silly. I'd really miss my tail."

"Me too." Peter flicked his tail so that it lay next to the lion's huge stone one. "Thank you for looking for rats with me."

"I just wish we'd found one." Tasha shook her whiskers. "Where are they all? That's what I want to know."

"You two had better not fall asleep up there!"

Peter and Tasha popped their heads over the lion's paws and peered down at Ivan. The old white cat was sitting in front of the statue, gazing up at them from under his huge furry eyebrows.

"There's a big party of visitors just about to walk by and you look as though you're settling in for a nap. Come on down."

"Ooops. Sorry, Grandpa." Tasha hopped off the pink lion to land next to him and Peter leaped after her.

"You can come and sit with me instead," Ivan suggested. "I haven't had a chance to talk to you yet, youngster."

Tasha's eyes widened and Peter glanced

at her worriedly. Old Ivan wanted to talk to him? Ivan was the oldest cat in the museum and a fearsome warrior. Boris had already boasted to him about his grandfather's amazing rat-catching exploits. What would such a famous cat want to talk to a skinny little kitten for?

"Make sure you shout in his left ear," Tasha hissed at him as they followed Ivan through a neat little doorway in the corner of the Egyptian Gallery behind the mummy case and trotted down the passage to the cellars. "He's deaf."

"I heard that, miss!" the old cat snapped back. "Not so deaf that you can get anything past me."

Tasha looked quite shocked and the two kittens went the rest of the way to the cellar den in silence.

"So you're befriending our new arrival, hmmm?" Ivan asked, once he'd padded himself a warm little nest in a pile of threadbare velvet curtains. He looked down at the two kittens sitting politely in front of him, his blue-green eye narrowing. "Making sure he knows his way around?"

"Yes, Grandpa."

"Good, good… And you, whatsyername…"

"Peter," Tasha put in helpfully and her

grandfather glowered at her.

"I knew that! Whatsyername, like I said, how are you finding the museum, hmmm?"

"It's very beautiful," Peter said nervously.

"My grandkittens looking after you properly?"

"Er…" Peter gave Tasha an anxious look. What should he say? Grandpa Ivan looked as though he could smell a lie at fifty tail-lengths, but he couldn't say that Boris was a bully and Bianca was just plain mean, could he?

"Hmmm. That ginger grandson of mine giving you a hard time, is he? Don't you listen to him, whatsyername. He'll be a loyal friend once you've won him over,

I promise you that. And as for Little Miss Bianca, she's not as feather-witted as she makes out."

"Grandpa," Tasha put in. "What's happened to all the rats?"

"What?" Ivan peered down at her. "What are you talking about, tabby-one-whose-name'll-come-to-me-in-a-minute?"

"We can't find any. We've looked everywhere. Do you think they've left? Maybe there aren't any rats in the museum any more?"

The two kittens stared at Grandpa Ivan and he stared back, wide-eyed. Then he started to make a strange wheezing coughing noise. Tasha and Peter exchanged worried looks, and then they realized. The old cat was laughing.

"I don't think it's funny," Peter whispered. "If the rats have left, the museum won't need cats any more. I think it's quite serious, actually."

"No more rats, a-ha-ha-ha-ha-ha! Oh, curl my whiskers. You two'll be the death of me." Grandpa Ivan wiped the end of his tail over his one watery eye and sighed shakily. "Dear ones, there are rats all over this museum. Everywhere!

You may not have seen them, but that's only because they're sneaky – and you aren't."

"Yes, we are," Tasha said crossly. "I'm ever so sneaky. I've got stripy camouflage. And Peter's a black cat – that's the best kind of coat for hiding. We're very sneaky indeed, Grandpa, thank you very much!"

❧ Chapter Eight ❧

"Not sneaky. Honestly," Tasha growled as they stomped away. Or rather, she stomped and Peter padded after her, not quite sure why she was so upset.

"Perhaps you'll be sneakier when you're bigger," he said, trying to be comforting as they popped up out of the hole behind the mummy case in the Egyptian Gallery. He snuffled a sneeze at the strange musty smell.

"I'm sneaky now!" Tasha mewed, glaring at him furiously. Then her whiskers drooped as she realized just how much noise she was making. "Maybe I'm not." She sighed. "Maybe Boris is right. Perhaps I do spend too much time making up stories. Maybe I'm not a proper hunter at all."

Peter looked at her, a bedraggled little cat with her ears hanging sideways and her tail sadly fluffed and he felt himself stand up straighter. "Yes, you are! We both are! We're going to find a rat, Tasha.

We are both brave and fierce. And who wants to be sneaky like a rat anyway? Come on!"

"OK." Tasha nodded excitedly, her ears perking up again. "It's nearly closing time. The rats come out when the visitors leave." She gave a little shudder and the hairs lifted up all along her spine. "Ma will notice when we're not back for supper, but I don't care. Which way are we going?"

Peter glanced around desperately. He hadn't actually got as far as working that out. Then he closed his eyes and tried to concentrate. Herring had said that his nose was exceptional. And the other cats were certain that there were rats all over the museum. So surely he should be able to smell them?

Tasha huddled closer to him as he sniffed the air. Somehow the gallery seemed to be getting darker and stranger with every passing moment. She did want to hunt out a rat. She did. It was just … she hoped it was going to be a small one.

Over on the other side of the gallery, a set of trembling whiskers emerged from a crack in the floorboards, followed by beady black eyes and twitching ears. Another rat appeared behind the first, and then another and another.

"Little cats," the first rat whispered.

"Very little."

"But tasty…"

"Fur gets in your teeth," the last rat growled.

Peter's eyes opened wide. "I'm sure I can smell a rat!" he whispered to Tasha, taking a few steps out into the gallery. "Or maybe even lots of rats," he added, sounding a bit worried now.

"Ohhh-ooooh…" Tasha squeaked. "I mean, oh good!"

Just then, the main lights clicked off – it was closing time. The two kittens blinked, but their night vision was good enough to see properly even in the dim emergency lighting. The darkness did make everything feel more serious, though. They were proper hunters now. The greenish lights shone here and there on the gold-painted mummy cases, but most of the gallery was in deep in shadow.

"Come on," Peter said. He was hoping that Tasha couldn't see how trembly he was feeling. But she so wanted to catch a rat and he was going to find one for her. He was sure he could smell them – in fact, he thought the scent was getting stronger.

Over on the other side of the gallery, the line of rats crept forward, their tails hissing over the boards.

"What was that?" Tasha asked suddenly.

Four rats froze…

"I didn't hear. Oh! Maybe I did…" Peter peered around. There was definitely a noise – but he couldn't tell where it was coming from. Somewhere outside the gallery? But the rats were closer than that, he thought. They smelled really quite scarily close… Should they follow the smell, or the noise?

"I'm sure it sounds like little ratty claws," Tasha said, hurrying towards the door.

Peter stood listening, his whiskers swivelling, ears pricked. "Yes…" he breathed. "You're right. I can definitely hear something creeping about."

The kittens hurried out of the gallery, following the rustly noises. Peter nodded respectfully to the bronze cat goddess in the case by the door and tried not to imagine that she was watching him go. Then again, she might be pleased with them. She probably didn't like rats either.

They pattered away into the Roman Room and four rats peered after them, whiskers bristling with disappointment.

"What happened there?" one of them muttered crossly.

"Our dinner went galumphing off, that's what happened."

"Four kittens now, did you see?" sniggered the largest rat. "Ginger, white, tabby, and now a black one as well. Too many little cats…"

All the rats nodded and muttered and hissed as they crept back into their tunnels.

Peter and Tasha were so determined to hunt down whatever it was making those rustly noises that they ran right over the feet of a statue sitting on the steps of the Roman temple – and then the statue woke up and muttered something about, "Dratted kittens everywhere!"

"Was that the Old Man?" Peter whispered as he and Tasha raced past.

"Yes, I told you he was grumpy. Usually he whistles so we know to avoid him. Never mind, he was half asleep. He has to keep walking round all the galleries to check for burglars, but he stops for a rest every now and then. I expect that means supper's going to be late. Ma might not even notice we've gone!" She paused, her ears swivelling. "Listen, can you hear it? That rustling again?"

Peter strained his ears. Yes… There was definitely something making scratchy little noises up ahead. But the strong ratty smell had died away. He was very confused, but Tasha seemed to know where she was going.

"It's coming from the Dinosaur Gallery, I think." Tasha nodded. "That makes sense. The Old Man likes to sit in the Dinosaur Gallery to eat his midnight snack – he leaves his sandwiches in a bag under the guard's chair – Boris is always sniffing around them, but Ma says he has to leave them alone. The rats are probably after the sandwiches too."

They crouched low to the ground and crept into the Fossil Room, every whisker shuddering with excited terror. Then Peter stopped, just before the door to the Dinosaur Gallery.

"What do we do if we catch one?" he whispered.

Tasha stared back at him, looking confused. "Um. I don't know. Maybe – call for Grandpa Ivan? Or Ma?"

"OK. Let's go then." Peter said bravely and shoulder to shoulder they tiptoed into the Dinosaur Gallery.

It was ghostly in
the faint lighting, with
the huge skeletons looming up
out of the darkness. The largest
one, the great apatosaurus, seemed
to be curling its huge neck down to peer
at the tiny kittens.

"I can definitely hear something now,"
Tasha breathed, and Peter nearly
squeaked with fright. He'd
been so busy side-eyeing the
skeletons, he'd almost forgotten
about her.

He gulped in a deep
breath and tried not to show
how scared he was. Yes, Tasha
was right. There was a soft,
quiet scrabbling up
ahead.

"Over by the
tyrannosaurus," Tasha
said, her tail flicking
wildly from side to side.
"Can you hear?"

"Yes. Is it a rat?"

"It has to be. I'm sure it's bigger than
a mouse." Tasha crept along beside the
apatosaurus's plinth and Peter padded
after her, ready to spring on the rat.

Tasha was definitely better at listening for strange noises than he was, but he was sure he could biff a rat round the whiskers – he was going to give it his best try, anyway.

"I can hear it now!" he whispered. There was a soft chomping sound and a squeaky rustle. Something was eating the Old Man's sandwiches!

"Hey!" Tasha mewed. "Leave those sandwiches alone, you nasty thieving rascal! They don't belong to you!"

Peter closed his eyes, let out a wild yowl and leaped forward, pummelling the rat with his paws. It was surprisingly big. Definitely bigger than he was. Luckily, it seemed to be so surprised by the attack that it wasn't fighting back. Yet.

Tasha was bounding about, trying to grab the rat's tail and uttering fierce little growls. "See! We're sneaky! We are! We got you, you sneaky rat! Don't you dare eat another mouthful!"

"Oi!" the rat yelled at last. "Get off! Hey, Tasha, get off my tail! What are you doing? I'm not a rat!"

Peter pulled back his paw, and peered at the rat in the dim light. It was furry ... and stripy ... and ginger...

Their rat was Boris!

🐾 Chapter Nine 🐾

"What do you two think you're doing, jumping on me like that?" Boris yelped. His ears were pressed flat against his head and his tail was three times its usual size.

He was just as scared as they were, Peter realized suddenly.

"This is all your fault, isn't it?" Boris glared at Peter. Now he'd worked out that he wasn't being set upon by a bunch of starving rats, he was starting to get angry.

"We weren't the ones stealing!" Tasha snapped back. "How could you eat those sandwiches, Boris? That's the Old Man's midnight snack! He'll be furious!" She peered into the little canvas bag where the guard kept his sandwiches. Boris had pulled it out from under the chair and the silver-foil wrappings were all undone. The sandwiches smelled wonderfully of ham.

Boris did look a little ashamed for a moment, but then he shook his whiskers and shrugged. "He'll just think it was a rat – like you did." He smirked at Tasha, showing his pointed teeth, and she hissed crossly.

"You're so – so – so stupid! The Old Man will see his sandwiches have been nibbled and he'll think that us museum cats aren't doing our job properly! That's Ma and Grandpa and the uncles and aunts … and they work so hard." Tasha's fur was standing on end, she was so cross, and Boris looked down at his paws. He obviously hadn't thought any further than wanting a delicious ham sandwich.

"I was trying to show Peter how to catch a rat and you've just spoiled everything!" Tasha went on, and Boris straightened up.

"Him! I might have known. Why are you bothering? He doesn't belong here. We don't need him."

Peter stepped backwards, nearly bumping into the tyrannosaurus's plinth. He had to put some distance between

himself and Boris – the ginger kitten
was only saying what Peter had said to
himself, but his words felt like sharp
scratching claws. They really hurt.

"Don't you dare run away," Tasha
snapped, whirling round. "Get back
here! I'm trying to prove you're a proper
museum cat and you just give up and
disappear!"

Peter stared at her helplessly. If one
kitten thought he belonged and one was
absolutely certain he didn't, which one
should he listen to?

"Look at him!" Boris jeered. "He's such a wimp. Can't he stand up for himself, Tasha? Does the poor little kitten need you to do all his fighting for him?"

"He knocked you over!" Tasha pointed out.

Boris decided to ignore that. "You're both useless."

"Hey!" Peter felt his whiskers bristle. He still didn't feel like a proper museum cat, but he knew Tasha definitely was one. And she'd been kind enough to try and help him. He wasn't going to let Boris call her names. "You don't get to say things like that – you're just a common thief. It's not enough taking more than your share at meal times, you have to steal food as well?"

"I'm growing!" Boris protested. "I have to eat more than the others."

Peter could hear Tasha squeaking with laughter and it made him feel taller somehow. "Maybe that's why you don't want another kitten around, because you're worried there won't be enough food! You're just greedy!"

"No, I'm not!" Boris yelled. He launched himself at Peter in a wild, flying jump.

And missed.

Peter and Tasha turned slowly to watch as Boris soared through the air. About halfway through the jump, Boris seemed to realize what he'd done and he tried to pull back. For a second he swam in mid-air, all four paws pedalling wildly. But it

was no good. A heavy, solid, really quite
large ginger kitten crashed right into the
tyrannosaurus's bony tail.

Boris hung there, scrabbling at the
smooth bones with his claws, and then he
dropped down on to the plinth, shaking
his orangey ears and peering dazedly at
the other two kittens.

"Are you all right?" Peter asked, putting his paws on the edge of the plinth and peering up at him.

"I think so," Boris muttered. And then he added, "Ow!" as a small bone fell on his head. "Ow! Ow! OW!" Another bone fell, and another, and another – until Boris was sitting in a small pile of bones and half the tyrannosaurus's tail had disappeared.

Boris shook himself and looked at the bones scattered all around him. "Ooops!"

"That's not good," Tasha said, putting her paws up next to Peter. "Oh, that's really not good."

Boris looked at her hopefully. "We couldn't just … sort of hide them behind the curtains?" he suggested. "Would anybody actually notice?"

"Yes!" Tasha glared back at him. "Of course they would. This is the most popular gallery in the museum – and this is the most popular dinosaur. I don't know why. It's got useless paws."

"I expect the visitors like the teeth," Peter suggested. This dinosaur did have absolutely enormous teeth, some of them almost as long as a kitten's tail. Was it his imagination or was the tyrannosaurus's head turned a little more towards them than it had been before? The long sharp teeth and the huge empty eye sockets seemed closer than they had been a moment ago. Peter knew the tyrannosaurus was only a skeleton, but he could have sworn that the massive dinosaur was not happy.

"So…" Boris poked the bones with his paw and they rattled together spookily. "You think we ought to put it back together? That might be a bit … tricky."

"You are such an idiot," Tasha

muttered, jumping up next to him to look at the bones.

"It's his fault." Boris nodded at Peter. "I was supposed to land on him. He moved."

"I didn't! You just missed by miles," Peter protested. "Anyway, why should I have to stay still and let you squish me?"

Boris shrugged. "I suppose you're right."

Peter jumped on to the plinth to join them. He peered at the pile of tail bits and then up at the big gap in the middle of the tyrannosaurus's tail. "It's all supposed to be held together with those wires," he pointed out. "We just need to thread the bones back on. In the right order."

"But there are so many," Tasha wailed.

"And the Old Man will be coming round soon."

"Then we'd better get on with it," Peter said grimly. It wasn't his fault that Boris had crashed into a dinosaur, but it wouldn't have happened if he hadn't been there. He didn't want to give the museum cats a reason to throw him out.

He blinked and thought about what that meant. The museum belonged to him too. He wanted to stay.

🐾 Chapter Ten 🐾

Tasha hopped down from Boris's back,
where she'd been balancing, and peered
up at the tyrannosaurus's tail with a
frown. She'd been threading tail bones
back together for what felt like hours.
Pretty soon the Old Man was going
to turn up – or Ma was going to come
looking to see why they'd missed supper.
She wasn't sure which would be worse.

"Are you absolutely sure there isn't another bone?" she asked Peter. "There's a hole in that tail. Just look."

There was – a big hole as well – right in the middle, where nobody was going to miss it.

"You stuck it together wrong," Boris said accusingly. "Ow, Tasha, you're too heavy. My bones are going to fall apart in a minute."

"We can always leave you to sort it out by yourself," Peter suggested. "Go ahead if you don't want us."

"I didn't say that," Boris muttered sulkily. Then he added, "Thank you for helping me," in a very fast whisper that anyone who wasn't listening carefully would have missed.

"What on earth are you three doing?"

All three kittens had been staring up at the gap where the missing bone should be. Now they whirled round in panic and another bone fell out of the tail on Boris's head. He was used to it by now and hardly even flinched.

Bianca stood by the side of the plinth, every hair perfectly in place, looking up at them in horror.

"Did Ma send you to find us?" Tasha asked, but Bianca wasn't listening.

"You broke an exhibit…!" She looked daggers at Peter.

"It wasn't Peter, it was Boris," Tasha said swiftly. "He banged into it."

"Oh… Surprise, surprise." Bianca glanced behind her. "But you have to fix it. Now! The Old Man's in the Egyptian Gallery, he'll be here any minute."

"We can't," Peter explained. "There's a bone missing. We've looked everywhere for it."

"This is even worse than the Old Man thinking we let rats eat his sandwiches!"

Tasha wailed. "This is a disaster. We never damage the exhibits, never, never, never. It's the most important rule!" She huddled down into a little ball and shuddered.

Boris was still sitting under the tyrannosaurus looking a bit dazed and Bianca was twitching her tail in panic. Peter laid his ears flat, thinking hard. They had only moments before the Old Man came by. Somehow, they had to disguise the big hole in the dinosaur's tail. "Maybe we can use something else to fill in the gap for now," he murmured.

"Something else like what?" Bianca demanded, looking around. "There isn't anything!"

"Something white, and about the size

of – the size of—" Peter broke off, staring at Bianca.

"What? Why are you looking at me like that?" The white kitten stepped back nervously.

Peter prowled towards her, eyeing her white fur. Bianca squeaked, twitching her fluffy tail away from him. "Leave me alone!"

Peter shook himself. "I'm sorry – I didn't mean to scare you. It's just – you're the same colour as the bones!"

Bianca scowled. "Yes, I'm a white cat. Obviously. I have beautiful fur. Is this really the time?"

But Tasha had looked up and was eyeing Bianca too. "She is! She's the same colour! Oh, Bianca, you can be the bone!"

"I beg your pardon?" Bianca said.

"She needs to hurry," Peter said, his ears stiffening up straight. "I can hear the Old Man whistling. Quick, Boris, shove his sandwiches back under the chair. We don't want him noticing that they've been moved. He needs to be in and out of this gallery as quickly as possible."

Boris made a wobbly jump down to the floor and pushed the sandwiches back. Then he sat by the chair, shaking his head from side to side.

"Is he all right?" Peter whispered to Tasha.

"He looks the same as normal to me," Tasha said. "Anyway, this is all his fault. He deserves to have a headache. We can sort him out later. Right now we need to get Bianca up there, somehow."

The Old Man's whistling was getting closer and closer, and the two kittens looked hopefully at Bianca. The white kitten glared back, her blue eyes haughty.

"I really don't know what you two are talking about," she hissed. "But I don't like it."

"We need you to be the missing bone," Peter explained. "You can hold on to the skeleton with your claws. It'll be easy, honestly."

"Just for a minute or so while the Old Man shines his torch over the skeletons," Tasha put in. "Otherwise he's definitely going to spot the hole."

"I don't look anything like a dinosaur bone!" Bianca said, horrified. "It's all manky and old and – and lizardy!"

"It's only for a minute," Peter pleaded.

"No!"

"Of course you don't look anything like a bone," Tasha said, gently bumping noses with her sister. "You're ever so much prettier. And your fur's all sparkly white, not yellowish like a bone. Oh, Peter, I don't think it's going to work! It's just impossible. The Old Man will never think Bianca's a bone. Not even Bianca could act that well." She saw Peter open his mouth to argue and dropped one furry eyelid in a slow wink.

"Oh – er, no. You're right." Peter sighed

heavily. "We're sunk. I thought Bianca was going to save us all, but it's just too hard, even for her." He glanced sideways at Bianca – were they being too obvious? But the white kitten was preening and fluttering her whiskers.

"I am a very good actress," she purred. "Perhaps I could try?" She stepped delicately on to the end of the tyrannosaurus's tail and walked up to the hole, sniffing disgustedly at the bones. "They smell…" she muttered. Then she hopped up on to the skeleton, gripped the wire tightly and twitched her tail to look as bone-shaped as she could. "There. How do I look?"

"Perfect!" Peter breathed. "You look exactly like a bone. Except much, much more beautiful," he added hurriedly.

"Just hold tight, Bianca," Tasha whispered. "The Old Man's coming. Boris, Peter, hide!"

The three kittens slipped away to the corner of the gallery and tucked themselves in the shadows behind a fire extinguisher. Peter and Tasha huddled together, shaking with nerves as the Old Man stomped in, waving his torch.

"I hope Bianca remembers to close her eyes," Tasha hissed worriedly, as the torchlight swept over the tyrannosaurus.

The torch passed over Bianca, then stopped and came back, and Peter's whiskers trembled. Had they been found out?

🐾 Chapter Eleven 🐾

But the torchlight passed on by and the Old Man kept on whistling – and then at last he walked away.

"We did it!" Tasha mewed. "Has he really gone?"

"Yes," Peter reported back from the doorway. "He's headed through to the volcano exhibit. We're safe!"

"Until he comes back," Bianca pointed

out. "Owww, my claws ache from holding on. This skeleton is very, very bony." She dropped down on to the plinth and shook out her paws delicately.

"You did so well," Tasha told her, purring and sniffing at her sister lovingly.

"But Bianca's right," Peter said. "We've only got – what, another hour until the Old Man comes round again? We have to find that bone."

"And we ought to make sure Boris is all right," Tasha remembered. "Boris! Where are you?"

"Here…" Boris mumbled. "I'm fine. Just a bit dopey. A lot of dinosaur fell on me, you know. Here, hang on, isn't that someone coming!"

All four kittens froze. Had the Old

Man noticed something odd after all?
Was he coming back to check?

But instead, an old white cat came
pacing through the doorway and eyed
them sternly.

"Grandpa Ivan!" Tasha purred, running
to brush her whiskers against his.

"Just what have you kittens been up
to?" her grandfather demanded.
"Your ma's off on her shift
guarding the museum so
she sent me to find out
where you all were.
You should be
asleep." Then his
gaze sharpened
and he
hurried over

to the tyrannosaurus skeleton. "There's a hole in this dinosaur!"

"There are a lot of holes in it," Boris pointed out cheekily, but then he ducked his head as everyone turned round to scowl at him.

"What happened?" Grandpa Ivan sighed.

"I might have … bumped it. Just a little bit," Boris admitted.

"So what happened to the bone?" Grandpa Ivan looked round as if he hoped to find it lying on the floor somewhere.

"We can't find it." Peter sighed. "We've looked and looked, but the bone just isn't anywhere." He glanced at Tasha. "Maybe a rat stole it?"

Grandpa Ivan snorted.

"You did say they were everywhere," Peter protested.

"They only steal things they can eat – or swap for more food. I don't think any sensible rat is going to want a bit of tyrannosaurus tail. No, it must be here somewhere." The old white cat strolled all round the plinth, sniffing thoughtfully. "I can smell ham," he said at last, stopping to sit down in front of the kittens with his puffy white tail wrapped around his paws.

"It's the Old Man's sandwiches," Tasha said, glaring at Boris. "That's what started all of this."

"They do smell so good." Boris sighed and Bianca narrowed her eyes.

"You're dribbling, Boris. Stop it."

"I can't! I'm hungry. Couldn't I just eat the rest of the sandwich that I started?" Boris looked hopefully at the others. "It's already got one corner nibbled off. So really it would be better if I ate it all up. Don't you think?"

"No," chorused Tasha, Peter and Bianca, but Grandpa Ivan pricked up his ears.

"So … you opened up the sandwiches?"

Boris hung his head sadly. "I couldn't resist it. Sorry, Grandpa."

"And that was before you launched yourself into this dinosaur?"

Boris's whiskers were practically trailing on the floor now. "Yes," he whispered.

"And you've looked everywhere for this bone? All of you?"

The four kittens nodded. They really had.

"It isn't anywhere," Tasha said, shaking her head crossly.

"It's in the sandwich bag, you silly kittens!" Grandpa Ivan got up, and used one paw to hook out the canvas bag and flip it open.

There, on top of the sandwiches, was the missing bone, gleaming palely in the moonlight.

"You found it! You found it!" Tasha squeaked, dancing around the sandwich bag, and Grandpa Ivan yawned widely as if it had all been very easy. But his eyes were sparkling and Peter suspected that he was actually rather proud of himself.

"So, when we told Boris to put the sandwiches away – the bone was there all the time? Boris, didn't you see it?"

Boris shook his head slowly. "No... But I wasn't feeling very bright at the time. I suppose I could have missed it. Er – sorry, everyone..." Then he caught Tasha's eye and sidled up to Peter. He rubbed his face apologetically against the black kitten's neck. "I shouldn't have said those things, about you being skinny... And not belonging here... It was mean."

Bianca nodded. "If you hadn't thought of me pretending to be a bone, the Old Man would have caught us for sure. Of course, it all depended on my brilliant acting skills, but it *was* a good idea."

Grandpa Ivan stared at her thoughtfully and her whiskers drooped. "And I'm very sorry I was mean," she added, shuffling her paws.

Grandpa Ivan glanced into the moonlight shadows and out through the doorway. "There's a little time before the Old Man comes back. First we'd better mend this dinosaur." He peered up at the skeleton thoughtfully and then stood creakily on his hind paws to nose the bone back into position. The kittens watched admiringly as he twisted the wires with his teeth, then sprang back down. "There. Poor old thing. No more messing about with bones, you hear me?"

"Yes, Grandpa," the four kittens chorused.

"Good. Now come, you kittens. Sit up here with me." He led them across the Dinosaur Gallery to a nest of fossil dinosaur eggs and settled the kittens in between the huge stones. "I want the whole story. Just what exactly have you been getting yourselves into since young whatshisname arrived?"

❧ Chapter Twelve ❧

Grandpa Ivan shook his whiskers sadly.
"You are a bunch of very silly kittens." He
sighed. "Of course whatshisname – Peter
– should stay."

"I told you." Tasha barged the black
kitten with her shoulder.

"I think I'd like to stay!" Peter said
shyly. "I like it here, I've decided.
I'm going to be a museum cat when

I'm older." His ears pricked up eagerly. "I might even ask if I can guard the dinosaurs, now I know how to put one back together."

"This museum is a haven for all cats," Grandpa Ivan said, eyeing Boris and Bianca sternly. "Have I never told you how I came to be here?"

All three grandkittens stared at him in surprise. "Weren't you born here, Grandpa?" Tasha asked. "I thought you'd been here forever. Oh, you know what I mean," she added, when the other kittens sniggered.

"It feels like I have been, when the wind's in the east and there's a draught blowing through the cellar making my old bones ache. But no. I came here as a kitten too." He leaned down to brush his whiskers over Peter's nose and the little black kitten purred with delight.

"I wasn't much older than you. I came from a village, further up the river, but I was too young to remember much about the place. Only that there was a barn and a tabby cat who was my mother." He sighed. "White cats are often deaf, you know. Oh, don't worry, Bianca. I know quite well that you can hear chicken hitting a dish at two hundred tail-lengths. But I think that's why they did it."

"Did what?" Peter nestled closer to the

old cat. His creaky voice sounded so sad, the black kitten wanted to comfort him.

"They wanted rid of me, you see. The people there. They must have thought I would be deaf and no good at earning my keep. So…" He glanced down at the four small kittens and hesitated, as though he wasn't sure he should go on with his tale.

"Tell us, Grandpa," Bianca whispered. She sounded quite different – small and scared, not the proud kitten she usually was. She crept closer to her grandfather too, and Ivan lay down, curling himself around the four kittens and licking Bianca's nose.

"They threw me in the river, tied up in a sack."

"No!" Peter squeaked, and the other

three kittens mewed in distress.

"I was supposed to drown, but for some reason I didn't. I floated instead and a child playing on the bank of the river fished me out. Since she wasn't far from the museum, she brought me here. And I became a museum cat. So you see –" he leaned down to touch noses with Peter again "anyone can belong to the museum, like I said." He purred a little chortle. "Especially if they're good with bones. Now, I promised your ma I'd find you and bring you back home, since it's so far past your bedtime that it's almost time to get up. The Old Man will be back here on his rounds in a minute or two. Off you go. Promise me you'll go straight to sleep."

"What are you going to do, Grandpa?"
Tasha asked as the four kittens padded
through the dinosaurs to the doorway.

"Ah, just going for a little wander…"
her grandfather purred. "My own rounds,
you know. Make sure all's safe. A museum
cat never really retires, you'll see…" He
sniffed thoughtfully and his eyes glittered,
and a large brown rat darted back
behind the stegosaurus skeleton, looking
worried.

"I'm going to be like your grandpa,"
Peter said as he followed Tasha down
the tunnel to the cellar. His tail was high
and proud and he felt like prancing. "A
great museum cat, even if no one knows

where I came from."

"Poor Grandpa was shut up in a sack," Bianca muttered, shaking her ears and shuddering. "A horrible wet sack. I should be braver, instead of fussing so much about my fur."

"If you didn't have beautiful white fur, you couldn't have saved us earlier on," Peter told her.

"Mmm. Maybe." But Bianca wrapped her white tail around his thin black one, just for a moment.

"Do you think we'll have adventures like Grandpa Ivan, one day?" Tasha sighed. "He's so brave."

Peter nudged noses with her gently. "We just did, Tasha. We mended a priceless dinosaur skeleton. And we did it all without anybody noticing."

"I suppose we did," Tasha agreed. "And we caught a sandwich thief." She glanced over at Boris, who looked a little ashamed of himself. Although not nearly ashamed enough, Tasha thought. "Do you think we'll have *more* adventures?" she asked.

"Of course we will!" Boris told her, brightening up a bit.

"But no more pretending to be bones, please," Bianca said sternly as she sprang up on to their tapestry bed. "It's undignified, even if I did save the day. Besides, Ma said to me this morning that it's time we had more rat-hunting lessons. We'll be far too busy for mending skeletons if we're learning to hunt."

"Night then," Peter yawned, twitching his paws ready to jump into the jewellery box.

"Aren't you sleeping up here?" Boris asked gruffly, looking down at Peter from the battered old tapestries.

Bianca nodded. "It's chilly tonight. You'll be cold in that box."

"And you're too big to fit in it," Boris added. "Not as big as me, of course. But not far off."

"Oh…" Peter's eyes brightened. "Well, if there's room."

He jumped up after the other three, and burrowed in between Bianca and Tasha. The four kittens wriggled comfortably for a while, padding at each other, so that Bianca's fluffy white tail covered Peter's nose, and Tasha's paws were wrapped round his neck. Boris was on top of him, like a furry ginger quilt, and every time Peter breathed, all four kittens went up and down.

When Grandpa Ivan padded back down the staircase, they were fast asleep, dreaming of dinosaur bones and rats and the adventures yet to come…

The Real Museum Kittens

This story was inspired by the cats at two museums. There have been cats at the Hermitage Museum in St Petersburg, Russia, since it was founded in the 1700s. Now about fifty cats live in the cellars of the museum, and sunbathe in the courtyards.

For years the British Museum in London had cats too. One of the most famous was Mike, who arrived at the museum as a kitten, carried in the mouth of a museum cat called Black Jack.

No one knew where the little kitten had come from, but Black Jack trained him up and he went on to guard the doors of the museum for twenty years.

Sadly, the museum no longer has any cats – except for the beautiful cat statues, jewels and mummies in its galleries.

Read on for an extract from Book 2

The Pharaoh's Curse

"What are they all so excited about?" Boris whispered to Peter and his sisters. He was peering round the huge, painted mummy case that hid the tunnel down to the cellars, where the museum cats lived.

The Egyptian Gallery was full of museum staff, talking in whispers as they opened up a large packing case and started to unwrap something that had been inside. The elderly professor who ran the Egyptology department was actually squeaking with delight.

"Is it jewels?" Bianca asked hopefully, pushing the large ginger kitten out of the way so she could see.

"It could be one of those golden masks that the pharaohs had in their tombs,"

the small tabby Tasha suggested, slinking
further round the mummy case to look.
"It must be something very special."

"Gold…" Bianca purred. "Diamonds
too? Maybe pearls?"

"I don't think so," said Tasha. "The
masks are mostly gold and lapis lazuli
– that lovely blue stone. The ancient
Egyptians used it a lot."

"Hmf! Blue stone." Bianca looked
disappointed and her white tail drooped.
"Not as nice as diamonds. But I do like
gold."

"*That* doesn't look like a jewelled
golden *anything*," Peter pointed out. The
black kitten had given up trying to see
round Boris and crawled underneath him
instead. "It's just … a bit of paper."

"Huh? That's not a treasure!" Bianca said crossly.

"What are you lot looking at?"

All four kittens skittered sideways in surprise as Grandpa Ivan appeared behind them. He was the oldest of the cats, white and long-haired with a great drooping moustache of whiskers, his ears looked chewed and he only had one eye. But he knew everything that was going on in the museum and he was very good at sneaking up on the kittens. "Ah, it's arrived then!"

"Do you know what it is?" Boris asked. "It doesn't look very exciting but the museum people are making a lot of fuss about it. They're putting it in an enormous glass case, look!"

"It's a temporary loan from a museum on the other side of the country," Grandpa Ivan explained. "They're rebuilding their Egyptian Galleries so they're lending out their precious exhibits. It's part of the Book of the Dead."

"The what?" Tasha squeaked.

"The Book of the Dead." Grandpa Ivan chuckled. "It's a set of ancient magic spells for how to get safely to the afterlife, written out on great long strips of papyrus. That's paper made of reeds, you know."

Tasha nodded intelligently and the other kittens tried to look as though they knew what he meant too. All four of them were gazing at the strange piece of paper in fascination. Ancient magic spells!

"The Egyptians used to put copies of it into people's tombs so the spirits would know what to do. The scrolls were expensive, though, so they were mostly made for royalty and important officials. This one came from the tomb of a pharaoh, Thutmose I, so it's very grand, with beautiful pictures. This isn't the whole thing, of course. Only a little bit of the scroll is left. All the tombs were raided by thieves many times – and you can imagine that a long roll of papyrus is quite delicate."

"Hang on… This is a list of instructions for *ghosts*?" Boris looked shocked.

"Mmmm, not quite. I think they'd only be ghosts if they got it wrong," Grandpa Ivan said thoughtfully. "Mind you, no one's quite sure where Thutmose I's body ended up… He had at least three different coffins. But what's really special about this bit of papyrus is that no one knows what it means. Most of the Book of the Dead has been translated – it's all written in hieroglyphics, you know. Picture writing. But this part of the book is tricky to read, apparently, and this is the only copy that's ever been found! I heard the staff talking about it in the café. They're pretty sure it's a spell to do with a magical amulet – or it could be a curse on anyone who steals it…"

"I don't like the sound of that," Peter muttered, his whiskers shivering. "What if it's bad luck for it to be here in the museum?"

"There's no such thing as bad luck!" Tasha gave him a grown-up sort of look. No one was exactly sure how old Peter was. He had been left at the museum as an orphan, so the other kittens liked to think he was the littlest. "Spells and curses are all nonsense. And even if they weren't, this one is thousands of years old! Its power must have run out by now."

"Or it's spent years and years getting worse and worse," Boris growled, and Peter nodded at him, round-eyed.

Tasha sighed. Really, the other kittens were all so superstitious. She knew there was absolutely nothing to be worried about…

HOLLY WEBB

Holly Webb started out as a children's book
editor and wrote her first series for the
publisher she worked for. She has been writing
ever since, with over one hundred books to
her name. Holly lives in Berkshire, with her
husband and three children.
Holly's pet cats are always nosying around
when she is trying to type on her laptop.

For more information
about Holly Webb visit:

www.holly-webb.com